bed on fire

The East Greenwich Fire Co. Series
Book One

maite maxwell

PARAMOUR
INK

introduction

Welcome to On Fire: The East Greenwich Fire Co. Series!

I'm Maite Maxwell, and this is my short romance series full of hardworking everyday heroes who fight for love, no matter the cost.

If you're searching for a steamy short read dedicated to fine-looking single dad firefighters who would do anything for the women who have captured their hearts, plus a little suspense, a lot of heroism, and plenty of much-deserved spice, you're in the right place.

If you want to read a bonus scene, become an advance-copy reader, or join my well-loved street team, sign up here: Maite's Newsletter!

content warnings

Bed on Fire is a short read, not a full-length novel. Hopefully this is the perfect reading length for you, because you're busy? Please don't get mad.

There is explicit sex and profanity within this story. If this content is too mature for your age, or you're not interested in reading about sex, you might want to try another story. Luckily, there are so many amazing reads out there waiting to be discovered!

This story contains passing references to death due to gun violence, trauma, PTSD, and the symptoms and effects of untreated, undiagnosed mental illness due to extreme grief. This book *actively* depicts unresolved grief, stalking, and physical assault. If it's not healthy for you to read about these topics right now, please stop here. We all love you and we want to see you happy and thriving. My other stories in the On Fire series do not feature stalking or assault—try one of those!

The aforementioned content does *not* transpire between, nor is it the result of the relationship between the main characters of this book, and this is not a dark romance. Within these pages, there is no deliberate abuse, bullying, BDSM, cheating, or abject sorrow (there is quite a bit of sorrow, actually, but it's not *abject*).

This and all my On Fire stories feature a happily ever after following a good dose of spice, suspense, and on-page strife.

I hope you fall in love with Kiki and Brock and the tiny town of East Greenwich!

xoxo,

Maite

*For **him**.*

prologue

. . .

Kiki

I SLAMMED the door shut behind me, threw my purse on the kitchen bar, and made a beeline for the bathroom to wash my hands and curse Sophie's name.

Sophie was great, indispensable at work, we'd gone from zero to close friends and confidants in less than a New York minute. *And* she'd helped hook me up with this amazing apartment. But the men she had in mind for my Friday nights left a lot to be desired. This was the second time I'd bitten on her lure, which, now that I thought about it, was pretty much, "Hey, I know a guy you could have dinner with." Not the most glowing reviews or marketing. And we worked at an ad agency, for fuck's sake.

I washed my face and took a good long look at

myself in the mirror. Why did you put up with that nightmare of a date? Mirror me didn't know either.

Over the course of a very short dinner, Jonathan had consulted three different screens, explained cryptocurrency at length, asked me if I "wanted in on the ground floor," and never asked me a single question about myself besides.

What a con artist. Maybe it wasn't even a date. Maybe it was a pitch session. I should have gotten the hell out of there, not entertained that crap for a whole hour. And then split the bill.

This miserable evening could only be salvaged by my Friday night glass of wine, and by masturbating the memory of this horrible date out of my mind.

Manhattan was tough. The work wasn't easy, and the dating was even harder. But I was tougher.

At least I had this great apartment. That was one thing Sophie had hooked me up with for sure. And I was grateful as hell. Her older brother had a friend in real estate, who'd let this place go at a steal. Otherwise I'd never have been able to afford to move from New Jersey to the Upper East Side. My three-hour car to train to subway across town to subway uptown to walking commute had been cut down to a beautiful 32-minute stroll through the greatest city in the world, thanks to her and her brother's friend.

My phone buzzed.

> I had a great time tonight. Let's do it again soon

I bet you did. Listening to yourself talk for 60 minutes was your dream date. And it didn't cost you a thing.

I stripped off my clothes and turned on the shower.

My phone buzzed again.

> Hey, what are you up to tonight

I didn't recognize the number.

> Who is this?

> Rob

Oh. My landlord. Sophie's brother's friend.

I didn't expect to hear from him. I was all paid up on the rent.

Was he asking me out?

I'd only met him once, to hand over the deposit

and first month's rent. Sophie said he was some kind of hedge fund manager, and his dad had made a fortune in property back in the day. So he had a few apartments "to play around with" from dear old dad.

I got in the shower and soaped myself up, trying to wash away the bad date and now, a weird feeling I had about this landlord text. I wasn't trying to date my nepo baby landlord.

Was that why he'd let me rent it for such little money? Because he wanted to date me?

I had to get this ick off of me: crypto bro ick, landlord ick.

And what was the best way to do that?

To get off.

I put one foot up on the side of the tub, licked my finger, and circled my clit. I searched my mind for any little scrap of real-world hotness, but I'd spent the week at work, as usual. There wasn't anything about advertising executives that made me wet or weak in the knees.

Ooh, sir, the way you wrote that catchy jingle to manipulate people into buying a product, mmmmm—

I had to give up. I wasn't getting anywhere with this solo session. I was so turned off there was no way of turning me on.

Pathetic. I couldn't come up with one masturba-tion-worthy man I'd met, after a year and a half of working in New—

Hey. What's that?

What *is* that?

I'd never noticed, in all the times I'd been in this bathroom, that there was, like, an extra smoke alarm or carbon monoxide detector stuck behind the door. I noticed it now because the light glinted off its power LED in the weirdest way.

In fact, it didn't even look like an LED.

It looked more like a lens.

prologue

. . .

Brock

"DADDY, I WANT ICE CREAM!"

"Okay kiddo, let's go and pick up some ice cream."

"I want the good kind from Martin's. Tommy at school said he always gets to have the good ice cream from Martin's in Salem."

I take a deep breath. It's been a long week down at the station. But I'm not going to use that as an excuse to lose patience with my kid.

"Do you remember why we don't go to Martin's?" He's too young to have any memories of that night.

"Because we like to go see Mr. Skelly at his store."

"That's right. His ice cream is just as good as Martin's. Tommy might be bragging a little. Next time he tells you about the good ice cream at Martin's you can tell him about the good ice cream from Skelly's."

"Okay." His face looks solemn now. "Daddy, what are we going to do on Sunday?"

Mother's Day. The only day I dread even more than the anniversary of her death.

"We're going to go visit nana and pop-pop. And we'll finally get to see their new baby lambs. Won't that be fun?" I ruffled his hair, admiring how adorable he was despite the absolutely terrible haircut I'd given him last week. "And maybe Nana will trim your hair up, too."

"Yeah."

I wonder if he's heard the other kids talking about their moms at school. About how they'll cele-brate Mothers' Day. Of course he has. Maybe he's protecting me.

"Daddy, are we going to go visit Mommy for her special day?"

"Do you want to bring her some flowers?" I turn away from him and run the faucet. I pretend to need to wash my hands so he won't see the tears in my eyes.

I didn't know how much time and energy adults spent hiding their pain from kids until I became a widower and a single parent.

"Purple ones because that's her favorite color."

"That's right." I force the words out hard so my voice won't waver, won't break. "That was mommy's favorite color. Let's go get that ice cream now and maybe Mr. Skelly will know where we can get some purple flowers."

I know I'll eventually have to tell him. He asks about her sometimes, about how she got hurt in an accident and went to heaven.

I never tell him the accident was a shooting, a failed robbery. He's too young. So I never say what really happened: Hailey was shot seven times at Martin's in the *only* violent crime this area has known in decades.

He had been in the car outside when it happened. Not yet one year old.

The whole thing was my fault.

And that's why we don't go to the Martin's in Salem.

one

. . .

Kiki

CLASSIC FRIDAY NIGHT in East Greenwich: just me and a glass of wine in my bathroom. I had so little to do, I decided to shave my legs for fun.

Not like anybody's going to see or touch them anytime soon. It's for the best, though. I have to keep reminding myself. I moved away from New York City precisely for this, moved here to get away from *him*.

I took another sip of the cheapest Shiraz in this tiny town and—*whoops*! Dribbled a little bit onto my favorite nightshirt. Right down the middle of this hole-ridden relic of my childhood. But I can't give it up: it's my emotional support nightshirt. Every girl needs one.

Good thing it's a party of one in here.

I made it midway up my calf, hard at work on Operation: *Hair Removal*. It's steady as she goes with that razor even though this isn't my first glass of wine: up, up, up…

An ear-splitting blast tore apart my concentration. I jumped. My hand jerked. I dropped my razor into the tub.

It's the fire alarm. *My* fire alarm.

Thick smoke wafted in from underneath the door. The only way out was on the other side of my apartment.

I yanked the door open.

Then I remembered you're never supposed to do that in a fire.

But there was no other escape.

I couldn't see anything. I groped my way around the apartment. I struggled to breathe, my lungs and chest on fire.

I'm going to die in here.

"Fire Department! Is anybody home?"

He sounded close, but I couldn't see him through the smoke.

"Help." I managed to choke out the word, strangled and suffocating, a croak he surely couldn't hear. "I'm here."

Strong arms scooped me up off my feet. I

couldn't stop coughing. Couldn't catch my breath. *I can't breathe*, I tried to tell him, but my lungs burned so hard the words died in my throat.

The heat seared my face and my feet and my eyes stung so awful I forced them shut tight and I clutched that firefighter with all the strength I had.

"I'll get you out of here."

———

I woke with a start, and tried to run from the fire. But my legs wouldn't work. Because I was being held up off the ground by a fireman.

Oh. We were outside.

He pressed an oxygen mask to my face. I heard sirens in the distance.

"Ma'am," my fireman says.

My thoughts came to me very slowly, like after the time Rob choked me out. Slow and scattered. But I was pretty sure this guy was the same one who broke in and rescued me.

I would recognize the feel of those arms anywhere.

"We didn't die in the fire," I said, just to verify.

"Nope. I said I was gonna get you out of there. Do you remember?"

"You did." I rested my head against him, fighting a new wave of dizziness. "You did say that."

The way he's holding me, cradled like an infant, I'm mortified to see my left leg is still covered in shaving cream. I can see it because it's bare. Not only that, it's also bleeding all over the place from where I'd nicked myself a good one when the alarm went off.

I can see all this because I'm not wearing any damn *pants*.

And what *am* I wearing? My ancient and hole-ridden emotional support cat nightshirt.

I craned my neck to see behind him. My apartment was still on fire. Three other firemen ran past, reeling their hose into the building. The sirens were getting closer.

Hopefully it's a small, quickly extinguished fire. I need to get back in my place tonight, or I've got nowhere to go.

And I can't lay around on this guy all night. No matter how big and strong these arms are. He's probably disgusted by my lack of hair-removal. But, hey, at least I was trying.

A few people gathered to watch on the opposite side of the street. My face went hot with rage and embarrassment. Then again, a small fire is probably the most exciting thing anybody in this town's got going on.

I tore off the oxygen mask. "Don't judge me."

Wait. Is somebody over there recording us on their phone?

I ducked my head into his chest, hiding my face.

"I would never," he said.

Is he flirting?

He was handsome in a way that made me want to put on a pair of pants so I could crawl into a hole without scraping up my knees and my hairy legs and then die in there of embarrassment. I hadn't noticed before now: his chiseled jawline, the corners of his big brown eyes crinkling behind the visor on his fire helmet.

Oh, he was judging me, alright. That smug smirk on his face said so.

"Great," I said. "Don't judge me because of this —," I pointed to the gray cartoon tabby on my faded junior miss nightshirt, "—or this—" I held up my leg, thick with months of uninhibited growth since I'd moved to the tiny town of East Greenwich, plus one bald strip down its center, peaking at my knee in a streak of blood mostly stemmed by his jacket, "—and definitely don't judge me because of what I'm about to say."

Normally I wouldn't be this forward with the

most attractive man I'd ever seen. And by far the most attractive man to ever hold me. But the smoke inhalation and the near-death experience and the oxygen made me bold.

"Of course," he said. I felt his voice against my hip. I wanted to focus more on panicking about my situation, but my brain just could not pull its shit together.

Not with him around.

I wondered if it was common practice to hold a fire victim in one's lap, or if not, how much longer I could expect this special treatment. He lifted his visor. His eyes were the color of a dark hot chocolate I wanted to drink, sweet and steamy, velvet over my tongue.

Kiki, *focus*.

"If those sirens are for me, I need you to call it off." I tried to put some authoritative oomph in my voice, but my throat was raw from yelling for help, and all the smoke, and I sounded shaky and weak.

"It's not a crime to have a glass of wine in East Greenwich." Those delicious eyes sparkled.

I cannot *believe* this is happening to me, that I am meeting the most incredible man I have ever seen on the absolute worst night of the lowest point of my life.

Well, not the worst. I shuddered, this time not from the cold—from everything I'd left behind.

Don't think about *that*. Not now.

Luckily my ADHD brain distracted me from the nightmare of my own recent past and forced me to notice this new development: my blood and shaving cream, I'd gotten all over his fireman jacket. I brushed at it with the back of my hand. Definitely wasn't coming off. Had already crusted. I wondered if they'd send me a cleaning bill.

"I hope not." What caused the fire, anyway? Please God, make it be one of those ancient appliances. Please, I need it to be something I'm not liable to pay for. Money wasn't a major player in my life right now, since I'd fled the city with little more than the clothes on my back. "And I hope that whatever *was* the source of the fire—"

"Bed's on fire," he interrupted me, deadpan. I couldn't tell if he was making some kind of sick joke about my lack of a love life or any Friday night plans, or what.

"*What*?" I tried to remember if I'd lit the candle in my bedroom or not, but I couldn't think straight with those tree-trunk biceps around me.

"We got a call about a bed on fire. And it's not the cops that are coming. It's an ambulance. For you. Aren't you the one who called us?"

I wasn't. "Oh, wow. Listen—" I choked and cleared my throat. "I'm fine. I feel fine now." I put one hand on his chest. Was he wearing some kind of steel under this jacket, or was that all...*him*? "Please. I can't afford to go to the hospital. And I sure as hell can't—oh *no*. My phone, my clothes, all my stuff..."

Everything I had was in that apartment, getting smoked to high hell at a bare minimum, if it wasn't turning to ashes right this minute.

"Okay. First things first. The boys'll do what they can to save your things and your place. You can refuse the ambulance. And we've got enough oxygen in these tanks to clear out your lungs from all that smoke. But I really think you should go get checked out."

He stood up, taking me with him, and he put his knee up on the bumper of the firetruck to balance me on it, and pulled out his phone from his back pocket with his free hand, handed it over to me, then sat down on the back of the truck. Still holding me. Like we were an act in Cirque du Soleil. "You got somebody you want to call?"

I stared at it dumbly, like I'd never seen a phone before. "No," I said. "I don't have anybody to call." The misery of my situation dawned on me. I'd moved to a tiny little town where I didn't know a single person. On purpose, of course, because of my situation. I couldn't call any of my friends back in New York on a local number. Then they'd know where I was, and what if they let it slip?

He'd be able to find me.

And who would I call in *this* town? Who memorized their landlord's number in case they burned down their apartment? Not this girl. Not me, with one strip of one leg shaved, sitting in the lap of a man who had the jawline of a god and the smile of

—*Kiki*, focus.

"Do you think I'll be able to get back in there tonight?" I tried to slough off some of the shaving cream on my leg with the back of my hand, but it stuck and hung there. I shivered and craned my neck to check out the progress on my place.

Smoke billowed out from my broken-down door. If it got any worse, my landlord's store underneath me would be gutted, and he'd probably have a thought or two about ever renting to an out-of-towner again. I shivered again. *Damn* it was cold outside when you weren't wearing pants and had shaving cream all over one leg. I was so screwed.

My fireman shifted me in his lap like I was no

more than a sack of potatoes and stooped to rifle through a bag on the ground, pulling out a foil blanket and crinkling it around me.

"Do you need a place to stay?"

two

. . .

Brock

"I'M GONNA GET RINSED OFF," My voice sounded panicked. I hoped she wouldn't notice, or chalk it up to a little bit of post-fire adrenaline.

Though the adrenaline coursing through my veins wasn't from the fire.

It was from *her*.

I hadn't thought through any of this. When I brought her back here. When I grabbed Hailey's robe where I'd left it on the back of the bathroom door since the day she died. When I gave it to Kiki.

I wasn't prepared when she emerged from the bedroom wearing it, wet-haired.

Stop being such a cliché.

There's no such thing as love at first sight. I'd said it when I took the oxygen mask off her, and finally let myself breathe at the same time Kiki did.

Besides the base level of fear that runs through a single parent's mind every damn day, the sheer terror that took hold of me when she lost consciousness was second only to the night Hailey died.

I couldn't explain it in any rational way, but I knew instantly that Kiki was *mine*, and I could feel it with my heart and my soul and *every* part of my body. She was here for me, and I for her. The moment she was in my arms, I knew I was put in this world to serve her.

I'd loved Hailey with all my heart. But this was something different. Something immediate.

Something fated.

Though, if you'd asked me yesterday, I would have said there's no such thing as destiny. I can't believe in fate, not after what happened.

Tonight I'm not so sure about that.

I avoided looking at Kiki directly and ran my fingers through my hair, still reeking of smoke. Normally I would have rinsed off at the station. Normally I wouldn't have taken a fire victim home.

It took all my self control to keep myself from pulling her back into my arms, here in my kitchen, and kissing her, this poor woman who had potentially lost everything she owned, and who was all alone in this world for some reason.

Well, I didn't know that. She was all alone in East Greenwich. But she'd moved here, what, two months ago? Nobody knew a thing about her yet. I'd heard Mrs. P spreading gossip at the pancake house last week. But I hadn't paid it any attention.

Now I wish I had. Because I was in love with her. Not love, I corrected myself. *Lust.* Maybe it was just post-fire adrenaline. Maybe I would have fallen in love with any woman who was wet and naked underneath my dead wife's robe. I hadn't had a woman in this house in five years.

"Thanks for the robe," she murmured. "Is this your....wife's?"

I pretended I didn't hear the question and ducked into my bedroom. Kiki had been through enough without watching a grown man cry tonight. "Be out in a minute," I called. "Make yourself at home." I tried to sound light, casual.

Sure, Kiki, we bring fire victims to our homes all the time here in East Greenwich. This is normal. Just being hospitable, ma'am. I'm not some desperate idiot widower who fell in love with you outside your burning apartment and then brought you to my house. And gave you my dead wife's robe.

I tossed my clothes into the hamper and hopped in the shower, my cock stiff with thoughts of her.

Not thoughts of *Hailey*. Of Kiki. The guilt hit me hard. A woman I'd known for a few hours. Not thoughts of my dead wife, mother of my boy, my only child, the light of my life. Not Hailey, whose robe I'd loaned away. Whose memory I'd been jerking off to for five years now, unable to conjure up even a smidgen of any feelings for another woman.

I could never stop loving Hailey. But could I make room in my life for another?

My heart raced around the memory of carrying Kiki in my arms, her arms wrapped around my neck, smoke and fire all around us, the cold dread from seeing Kiki in the oxygen mask, the flood of relief when she opened her eyes. Kiki, so ridiculously focused on her legs when she could have been burned alive in that damned deathtrap Old Jack Skelly pretended was an apartment, scraping her own blood off my jacket like we were going to send her a bill. Resilient in the face of all she'd lost.

So breathtakingly beautiful in that stupid cat shirt.

Afraid only of the cost of an ambulance ride. What a world.

Kiki in my kitchen, wearing Hailey's old robe.

Maybe I *was* ready to move on. But I wasn't ready to face Kiki in the kitchen. Because I couldn't get any harder. I could hang my towel on this erection.

Oh, Hailey. Forgive me. Give me a sign. Because I *need* to make room in my life for Kiki.

If she'll have me.

I leaned against the shower, turned the hot water up until it scalded me, and stood like that for a minute until my hard on subsided. But then I remembered Kiki in her damn cat shirt, and I got hard all over again.

I turned off the shower, toweled off, and swiped the steam off the bathroom mirror to see how bad I looked today. I ran a hand over my stubbled chin. Kiki wasn't the only one in this town who'd been neglecting a good shave.

It's okay. Nobody in this house needs to be hair-free. We were just in a fire, for Christ's sake. Nothing's going to happen tonight.

This is the plan: Find her some clothes to wear—

Her lips against mine.

—cook her a little dinner—

My tongue on her breasts, sucking each nipple until she moans.

—and let that girl get some sleep. Nothing is as exhausting as your first crisis.

Although, it's obvious she's already been through some shit, isn't that right?

My face between her thighs.

Not a great way to put a halt to this erection.

Then I recalled the look Jonesy had given me when I'd helped Kiki refuse the ambulance and carried her over to the passenger side of my truck. The look that said, What are you doing?

The look that said, You're cheating on my dead sister.

The look that said: If only *you'd* gone to the store that night instead of her.

And it was true. My stomach clenched, and my face got hot with the shame and the pain of losing Hailey all over again.

Nobody's qualified to judge you except you, I told the mirror. And you, I pointed at the ceiling.

"What?" Kiki hollered from the kitchen.

Oh *lord*. Had she heard me talking to myself and my dead wife in here?

Don't act like some lonely, lunatic, sex-starved loser, and definitely don't act like you just met the first woman who's made you feel anything worth a damn since your wife died.

Even though that's the truth.

Pull yourself together.

three

. . .

Kiki

HE CAME out of the bathroom, all heat and steam, in gray sweatpants and a white t-shirt that could barely contain him, and busied himself around the kitchen.

When he'd asked if I needed a place to stay, I'd assumed he meant a shelter or something. I didn't realize he was inviting me to an adult sleepover. At his house. Only him and me.

Well, him, me, and maybe whoever owned this women's robe.

A girlfriend? Didn't seem like a 'girlfriend' robe.

I guess he forgot I'm naked under here, under this robe. Get it together, girl. He's not interested in you, he's only doing the right thing by letting you stay here. It's small town logic. You wouldn't understand. You're a city rat, from your head, to

27

your heart, through to your aching, throbbing, totally untouched—

He stretched up to get something off the top shelf of an unfinished cabinet, and I couldn't tell if the rugged, woodsy smell was coming from him or the cabinet. When his shirt rose to reveal the chiseled lower abdominals of a man who had no problem carrying around a substantial woman like me, I wanted to shove my face into that hollow, trace my fingertips down that perfect line, and sniff his skin to find out for myself.

"I'm no five-star chef," he said. "But I can at least feed you. Got any food allergies?" He glanced back at me and frowned.

Suddenly self-conscious under his now-steely gaze, I pulled the mystery robe a little tighter up top. I still didn't know whose it was. Was there a Mrs. Brock? I must have looked like a total mess, even after my shower.

"You're bleeding."

Oh, wouldn't it be my luck to get my period on the same night my house had burned down and then bleed all over the floor of a kind stranger? A kind stranger whose arms had somehow been strong enough to carry me. Whose eyes made my insides quiver. My face reddened. I forced myself to look down, and let myself exhale. It was only my cut-up leg, dripping blood all over the floor.

"Just a flesh wound." I hoped I sounded cute and brave. Though it was bleeding quite a bit, and in a wide swath across my leg, starting right under the knee. I hadn't noticed the pain of it until now.

"Not on my watch." He winked. Then he swept out of the room.

All the adrenaline and panic of the night was finally wearing off. But the fluttery buzz around my heart and the growing throb in my core had ramped up.

Be an adult. One that's not lonely and sex-crazed.

I couldn't help myself. I ogled his thick thighs and perfect backside all the way out of the room.

When he was gone, my eyes settled on a crayon drawing on the refrigerator. Was there a Brock Junior?

He returned, carrying a good-sized first aid kit. Of course a fireman would have that in his—

My vision tunneled, from kitchen to darkness, and I stumbled forward.

"Easy there." Brock's strong hands caught me before I could break my nose open on his white kitchen tiles and bleed all over them a second time.

He held me tight with one arm and pulled a chair over to lower me down.

"I'm usually not…" I was so light-headed I couldn't even finish my joke.

He snapped into action, a medical army of one: testing my pulse with two fingers on my wrist, taking my blood pressure, slipping a sugar pill into my mouth, and a dozen other little movements he executed with a precision I'd never experienced at the doctor's office. I was too slow to stop him and say I felt fine. Maybe I wasn't fine. So I let him have at it. He seemed to really know what he was doing.

As usual.

He turned to me, stared deep into my eyes so intently it was like he could see inside my heart, and my soul—as if in one long look this firefighter knew me through and through. "I think you're hungry. And you're tired. And, let's face it: your bed burned down. And you're probably upset about it."

My bed burned down. Wow. That was the long and the short of my life right now. I laughed, in spite of it all. And then his stern expression broke, and he laughed too, which made me laugh more, which set him off, until we were both laughing so hard tears streamed down our faces.

"Thanks," I said. "I haven't really laughed in a long time."

"Me either." We both sat quietly for a long moment. "Can I clean up this cut?" He dug out the hydrogen peroxide and gauze from his kit and reached for my calf. I instinctively jerked my leg away from his hand. He trained those beautiful brown eyes on me and cocked an eyebrow. "I won't hurt you. I promise."

"Oh, I know. I trust you." And I was shocked to realize as soon as I'd said it, that it was true. I *did* trust him. After everything that had happened in New York. He was the first man I felt like being myself around. In a long time. "It's a reflex. It's, um, when I was really little I got this bad splinter, which shouldn't have been a big deal, and it wasn't. But for some reason it was this huge, traumatic event for me as a kid. So, my dad took it out for me. With tweezers, not, like, with a knife or anything crazy. In our kitchen, actually. Kinda like this. But, I guess, here's where the daddy issues come in—"

"I'll never understand why women get blamed for the failures of their fathers," Brock interrupted, with a quiet pain in his voice.

I paused. I'd never thought about it before.

Daddy issues. Who didn't have them? Seemed normal to me. I plowed on with my yammering.

"—he, uh, poured rubbing alcohol on it. It really hurt, and surprised me. I wasn't expecting it. And now I've got this weird reflex."

"It's not weird." His brow creased. "It makes perfect sense. He didn't have to hurt you like that."

"His idea of medical care, I guess. He was in the military—"

"I'm sorry, but I'm not going to sit here and listen to a smart, beautiful woman make excuses for someone who did wrong by her. I was in the military, too. Doesn't mean I would pour rubbing alcohol on a scared little girl's wound."

"You know, it was a different time."

He exhaled, sharp, almost a snort. "When, the early 2000s? There was no era when it was okay for a parent to break their child's trust. Especially when they were already hurting and afraid, Kiki. You deserved better."

For once in my life, I didn't have anything else to say. He kept his eyes on me and moved to pick up my leg, slow and careful, while I watched, mesmerized by his strong, powerful hands, settling my ankle onto his thigh.

And I didn't pull away.

He worked, methodically, gently patting the

blood away and disinfecting my cut, and then daubing on some triple antibiotic cream from the kit.

We were both silent while he bandaged me up. I became very aware of his fingers and the ropy veins of his hands, and how they felt on my legs, his measured breathing.

How close we were.

And how I was still wearing nothing under this robe.

four

. . .

Brock

I LEANED on the doorjamb only to physically stop myself from storming into her bedroom and throwing off those covers. I'd draped my grandma's quilt over her after carrying her to bed at 3 in the morning.

Give her some privacy. Don't be a creep.

Her hair splayed across the pillow, and the light from an abnormally bright sunbeam lay across her parted lips. Kissed them the way I wanted to. I wished I'd had the guts to kiss those lips last night.

I edged the door closed. If I looked any longer, my dick'd be standing at attention.

I imagined my face between her thighs, waking her up by tonguing her clit, my hands gripping her plush hips, holding her in my mouth as she bucked and called my name.

Too late. Time to retreat to my own bedroom. I'd gotten too hard, and she'd revealed a rough and tumble life last night that implied she might not want a stranger approaching her with his cock in his hand.

Last night had been perfect, and I didn't want to ruin it. Didn't want her to feel unsafe in any way. To think I was like all the other losers in her life, from her dad to her ex to the pervert landlord who'd been secretly recording her, and then, when she found out and tried to get away from him— turned violent and stalked her.

Fucking sicko.

Which was why she'd fled New York and landed in our tiny little town.

So I'd pushed any thoughts of touching her last night out of my mind.

And there were a lot of thoughts.

A lot. After she'd let me bandage up her leg, I was half-hard from touching her ankle. So embarrassing.

I finally found her some old clothes, one of Aunt Laura's old sets of pajamas from when she'd been staying at the house on Thursday and Friday nights with Ben while I was on the overnight shift.

Kiki's giggle turned into a snort from behind

the guest room door, and when she emerged and twirled to model them, we both laughed again.

"I don't know if I should be wearing these jammies," she'd laughed. "They're vintage."

"The eighties were an interesting time in fashion." But even hidden under my aunt's garish nighttime getup, Kiki's beautiful body was making me hard.

She didn't ask about the robe again. So I didn't have to tell her whose it was, after all. After she'd told me about her dad, and all that awful stuff about her landlord, I didn't need to dump on her with my own trauma.

We finished the night foraging cheese and crackers out of the fridge and hitting Aunt Laura's box of wine, much harder than I'd meant to, and talking for hours and hours, until Kiki couldn't keep her eyes open any longer. And she'd laid her gorgeous face down on my arm where it was slung behind her over the back of the sofa, looked up at me with those big, beautiful brown eyes, fluttered them shut, and passed out cold.

When I couldn't rouse her, I'd carried her to the guest room, slipped the quilt over her, and used every last bit of willpower I had in me to stop myself from kissing her forehead.

five

. . .

Kiki

I WOKE WITH A SPLITTING, boxed-wine-sized headache, groaning awake in a bed I didn't even recognize. The recent progression of events in my life and the succession with which I remembered them shocked me, in that it was all truly bonkers.

Oh, you left NYC and your hotshot advertising job.

Because your sick fuck landlord was recording you in your apartment and putting the footage online.

Then he stalked you into the suburbs.

So you fled to a tiny town you've never, ever heard of with basically the clothes on your back.

And the place you've been renting for the last two months caught on fire.

When you were rescued by the most incredible man you've ever met.

And you are waking up as hungover as you've ever been.

Because you were so nervously attracted to him you would not stop drinking his Aunt Laura's boxed wine.

I couldn't remember if I'd thrown myself at him or not. And I did not remember getting into this bed. But it wasn't his bed. I knew that much: I was in a guest room.

Maybe nothing had happened.

That realization hurt me too, and not just in my head: also in a sucker punch to the gut. *Why* hadn't anything happened?

It was a wild mix swirling around in me: shame and hope plus loss and dread. But when I thought about him, about Brock, I could only smile and enjoy the wild swarm of butterflies in my stomach.

I coughed, and it pounded the inside of my head so hard, I groaned.

"I hope you don't mind. I took the liberty of putting you in bed." He appeared in the bedroom doorway like a vision. Didn't look hungover at all. "You were really messing your neck up on my awful couch, but you wouldn't wake up for anything." He crooked his neck at a right angle to mimic drunk-me from last night. Behind my hang-over and my aching brains, I managed half a daydream about licking the part where his neck met his collarbone.

His thick black hair was still tousled.

But not from me. I hadn't touched it at all. My core throbbed only with emptiness and deep regret, not with the legacy of a badly needed delicious night exploring this man's body.

"Nothing, uh, happened." His eyes were wide, like I was frowning and miserable because he had laid hands on me. Oh no. It was the opposite. Really, I'd *wanted* him to lay hands and lips and tongue on me, and was full of regret only that I'd gotten shit-faced and passed out.

"I hope I didn't embarrass myself." I winced and clutched at my temples from the pain of speaking with this hangover. "I mean, any more than—" I swung my other arm wide to indicate the many reasons in my life to feel shame.

"Not at all." His lips twitched up at the corners. But he didn't reveal anything more about last night, or what he thought about me.

Maybe he didn't think about me at all.

I need to get this homeless lunatic out of my house, was probably what he was thinking.

Really, Kiki, there's no indication he feels

anything for you, any kind of attraction. You need to get a grip.

"Let me get you some coffee and…ibuprofen?"

I smiled, in spite of my pounding head. "That would be great, thanks."

I got out of bed to change and realized I still had nothing to change into. If he wanted these 1980s jammies back I'd have to return home in my smoke-damaged cat nightshirt.

And was there even a home to return to?

"I texted the boys down at the station." As if reading my thoughts, he called to me from the kitchen, over the merciful sounds of coffee brewing. "And they said your place is basically okay."

"Really?" A warmth spread through my chest. He was truly taking care of me, in a way nobody else ever had.

"Yep. They said it looked a lot worse than it really was. Seems like a bad electrical cord sparked and hit the bed. That comforter you had is toast, but all the smoke came from that, and the fire didn't spread. Old Man Skelly is hanging a new door, and he can put you up at his other place while he deals with the smoke damage, and all the cleaning. Probably be a week or two, tops."

"His other place?"

"Yeah, he's got a second store-plus-apartment in

town. Actually, it's right down the road from me. I can shoot him a text and drop you off there on my way to work. If you want."

I heard the clang of pots and pans, followed by the sound and smell of bacon sizzling and Brock's light, tuneless whistling. The domesticity of it all compelled me to stand in the doorway so I could watch. His broad-shouldered back was turned to me, so I could gawk at will like a love-starved idiot.

Yet my eyes were drawn to the crayon artwork on the fridge.

I walked over to get a better look. Two stick figures standing outside a house. Red brick, just like this one. Without thinking, I teased, "Did you draw this?"

And one stick figure in the sky, above the clouds. Plus a child's carefully spelled block letters: *MOMMY*. A mommy in the sky.

"I wish I had that much talent. Ben's handiwork."

The woman's robe, and who it belonged to, struck home. The ancient pajamas were left behind by Brock's aunt coming over to watch....Ben. I remembered the name now: Brock's son. I was a drunken moron. Suddenly Brock's nonstop hard work and self-sufficiency made sense. My heart swelled in my chest for him. Not only was he a firefighter, he was also a single dad, a widower, raising a son by himself.

When did she pass? I wanted to ask. But I didn't.

Brock had told me all about his son last night. The memory slowly seeped back into my brain from wherever it sat next to my end of the night blackout. I'd loved seeing his face light up when he talked about Ben. Little Ben, almost six years old. He was out of school for spring break, on a week-long fishing trip with his grandparents.

"It must be hard, being a single dad."

Brock had already scrambled half a carton of eggs and fried up enough bacon for a whole fire company, joined by the mouth-watering smell of toast on the way. I had to remind myself, this was how people outside the city lived: they cooked their own food, they weren't afraid of carbs. Fire-fighters ate normal things, like bread. They also rescued idiots from burning buildings for a living. And then housed them.

"Ben makes it easy. He's the best."

Something inside me broke: my inhibitions, my resolve not to throw myself at Brock like a fast-moving, big-city tramp without her stamp. (Yet.) I'd wanted the wine to propel me into his arms last night, but it had failed. Instead, my last straw keeping me from attacking this kind-hearted, noble, hardworking man was how he refused to complain about his life in the slightest.

"Hey, Brock?" I closed the distance between us and turned off the stove. I didn't want to burn down his house, too. "*You're* the best." He raised his eyebrows.

I couldn't lose momentum or I'd lose my nerve. I grabbed his thick, muscular forearms and wrapped them around me, my heart racing. I'd always been the pursued, never the pursuer. I threw my arms around his neck and pulled his lips down to mine. He resisted, at first, and my stomach clenched at the shame of rejection. But then he parted his lips for me, and let me in, and I slid my tongue along the length of his. I gently bit the soft skin of his lower lip when I pulled away.

I leaned back and put my hands on his chest to study his face for a reaction.

Surprise. Shock.

My stomach sank. This wasn't what he wanted, at all. I braced myself and waited for him to say: Listen. I was only being small-town-nice. Now get out of my kitchen, you crazy cat-nightshirt lady.

But he didn't.

His eyes narrowed, and he pulled me close until I could feel his thick erection pressed up against my stomach, his lips on mine, hot and wanting and seeking me out with a pent-up desire that matched my own.

He looked around and frowned. "Let's take this to the bedroom."

"Why not here in the kitchen?" I slid my hands into the waistband of his sweatpants to grasp his shaft. I thumbed his tip in small circles, swirling around the pre-cum. He gasped and closed his eyes, his hands in my hair turning to fists.

"I need you in the bedroom," he growled, and before I could answer he picked me up and slung me over his shoulder, smacking my ass. I yelped and took the opportunity to admire *his*, running my hands under his sweatpants so I could squeeze the powerful glutes working overtime to carry me into his bedroom.

Without another word, he cradled my head and neck, and lay me down on his bed so softly. He climbed up to hover over me, on his hands and knees, his massive arms bracketing me on both sides. He drank in my face with his eyes for a long moment.

Second thoughts, perhaps? I held my breath.

Then he violently tore off those garish pajama pants and buried his nose deep between my thighs.

I gasped. Much like the rest of me, it hadn't seen any grooming in months. I opened my mouth to apologize, but Brock's tongue found my clit at exactly the same time, and my apologies morphed into a long moan that he answered only with clipped grunts.

I braced myself on his shoulders and tilted my hips up. Otherwise I would have bucked so hard when his tongue hit rhythm on my clit, I'd have broken his nose.

It had been a long, lonely time.

I arched my back, moaning. He dragged my whole body closer to him, relentless with his tongue, and reached his hand up under my borrowed top to thumb my nipple, caressing my other breast with his whole hand. I flung my head sideways, hands in his hair—

—and stared right down the lens of a camera, red power indicator LED bright and gleaming.

My heart stopped beating and choked me in my throat. All my ecstasy shut down. The warmth in me died a cold death. The desire quickening inside me became a numbing fear in my gut. I planted my left foot on his shoulder and shoved back as hard as I could. It barely moved him, not an inch. But he stopped and raised his head.

"Did I—?"

I cut him off. "I have to go." My heart pounded so hard I was sure we both could hear it.

I need you in the bedroom. How could I have been so naive? This whole small-town-nice thing was a complete bullshit fest to get me in position and make more amateur porn.

I rolled off his bed and grabbed his aunt's pajama pants off the floor to step inside them while still moving, not stopping until I was back in the guest room, and I slammed the door shut. Not that it would do any good. There were probably cameras everywhere. Same as last time. Why was I a fucking magnet for psychos?

"Kiki? I'm sorry. I thought—"

I opened the door and blew past him in the kitchen, not stopping until I opened the front door and got outside the house, so I had room to escape, to run away—I didn't know where. Into the goddamned trees, I supposed, even though I was fucking barefoot. If it came to that. "I need to borrow these pajamas."

His mouth dropped open, incredulous. But that was how all discovered perverts looked when you found their hidden cameras and called them out on it. Rob had feigned that same I-would-*never* crap after I'd discovered the fifteen hidden cameras in the place he was renting me, thrown them all into the bathtub, smashed them to bits with a hammer, and turned on the tap. And texted him a picture.

So then he'd come by and thrown me up against the wall. Naturally.

The next six months of failing to escape him had been a living hell.

Which was why I had to get out of here *now*, without a word about the camera. Any man who could run the seamless deception Brock had for the past 12 hours wasn't safe to be around.

"Sorry." I couldn't keep the edge out of my voice, couldn't pretend I was actually sorry. I was never good at being fake or at hiding my feelings. "Just remembered I have an appointment." I looked down at my wrist, where I wasn't wearing a watch. "Can you give me a ride back to my place?"

He followed me out onto the porch. How is it that I fled my pervert stalker only to run into the arms of yet another pervert stalker?

"Kiki, what—" He cut himself off and clamped his mouth shut. He made a slight move towards me, and I flinched, and braced myself. Guess he finally realized I wasn't stupid enough to keep falling for his lies.

His whole body tensed, so mine did too. Based on the look on his face I couldn't tell if he was going to cry, or hit me. I took a step back, got down off his porch.

May as well make him work for it if he's going to come at me.

And then his expression changed, turned so miserable it aged him. His eyes weren't a deep brown after all. I'd been mistaken last night. High on asphyxiation and oxygen. This morning they looked gray in the light. The sun glinted off a streak of white in his hair I hadn't noticed before, either. I let myself exhale, shaky in my legs, still sopping wet from my desire, from his mouth on me. I'd almost fallen for it, for him. Just another liar-abuser-con artist to add to my list.

He sighed and rubbed his jaw. "Of course. I'll get the keys."

six

. . .

Brock

THE DRIVE over to Old Man Skelly's was the longest seven minutes of my life.

The night Hailey died, time had stopped completely. It only started for me again because I'd had Ben to look after.

This was different. This was me, driving away the best thing that had happened to me in the past five years. I didn't even know why. And I was powerless to stop it. Kiki was silent, but the expression on her face said everything. I'd messed up, *bad*. We still smelled of sex. She wouldn't even look at me.

When she got out of the truck she blurted, "I'll return these as soon as I can," and she slammed the door. Aunt Laura's ridiculous pajamas.

I sat for a moment to make sure she got inside the shop, and then I called Skelly.

"Morning, Loverboy."

"Not now, Skelly. Just making sure you brought over her stuff."

"Aye-aye, captain. Don't want your little lady without her phone."

"She's not little and she's not mine. Is Ellie taking care of her clothes?"

"Sure is, boss. Getting them de-smoked down at Reese's laundry as we speak. Loaned her some in the meantime. Everything alright?"

"Fine."

"You're not sore because of little Jenny Wallace's picture, are you? I'm sure the boys'll let you live it down someday."

Sore because of *what*? But I've been here in his parking lot for too long. Kiki's going to think I'm stalking her.

Stalking her. How could I be so stupid? Kiki told me last night about being stalked. How bad it got. Having to leave the city and secretly relocate way out here just to get away from him. Then, the next morning I threw her into my bed. Of course it triggered her PTSD.

But *she* kissed you.

She put *her* hands into your pants.

The memory of her hands on my cock made me twitch and ache for her.

"Brock? You there?"

I shifted the truck into reverse. Sitting here outside her place like a second stalker wasn't the right thing to do. "Yeah. I'm here, Skelly. What were you saying?"

"I was saying Laura told me you looked like a real American hero last night."

"How'd Laura see that?" I pulled over by the side of the road in one quick skid.

"Little Jenny took that pic of hers and put it on the neighborhood chat. And then Geena pulled it into the Gazette gossip page."

"What pic? Jesus Christ, Skelly. I gotta go."

Fifty-six unread texts in our cousin group chat later, I found the picture: first one from Jenny, captioned with a lot of emojis. Then one from Micah, this time on the neighborhood site. And finally, page 8 of today's Greenwich Gazette from Aunt Laura.

In the background, smoke streamed out of Kiki's apartment window and her shattered door. In front, the East Greenwich Co. fire engine. And me. Holding Kiki. In her cat shirt.

The caption read: Local firefighter rescues cat....lady.

Nobody reads the Greenwich Gazette. Kiki's face was visible, though. Not entirely, but—was it enough to be dangerous? I hammered the dash-board with my fist.

There was an online version.

Any psychopath with a reverse photo Google search could be here by the end of the day.

———

Back at the house, I breathed easier. Geena had already pulled down the online pic, and after a few stern words to Jenny I could hear the tears in her voice, gave up on my lecture about invasions of privacy, and told her I'd see her and her folks on Sunday at Jo-Jo's for tacos.

I had to restrain myself to keep from texting Kiki, from checking to see if she had her phone now, and if it worked, from making sure Skelly'd told her he would take care of getting her stuff cleaned. From making sure she was okay.

I wanted her to be okay, whether she ever spoke to me again or not.

I headed into my bedroom to get ready for work. But it smelled of her. Drove me crazy.

I sat down on the bed and went over the whole night and morning in my mind all over again.

I should have told her about Hailey right off the bat. Carelessly handing her that robe was a huge mistake. By the time I realized what I'd done, it was too late. I froze. Probably creeped her right out.

Here, have this random woman's robe I keep in my bathroom. I swear she isn't buried in the backyard.

Then I'd told her about Ben. She saw Ben's picture, pieced the whole thing together, obviously. It stank of desperation. Wanna be a substitute wife and mom?

Maybe she didn't even remember any of that. We had cut into Laura's box of wine pretty hard. What a dumb move. Bring a woman home from a fire, get her drunk, put the moves on her while she has nothing and nowhere to go.

Real romantic.

After she told you she'd fled a violent stalker.

Still, *she* kissed *you*. She squeezed your ass when you carried her into the bedroom. She ran her fingers through your hair while you licked her, soaking wet.

Oh, Kiki. She made me hard all over again. I took myself in hand, leaned back, remembered her moans, smelled her on my sheets. Imagined her hands in my hair, how she tugged on it. How her hips bucked when I tongued her hard and fast.

My eyes fell on the open closet door, and inside, an old security camera tossed on the shelf—the one I'd hooked up in Laura's yard last year with the motion sensor so she could see which wild animal ate all the cherry tomatoes out of her garden.

The camera wasn't plugged in. Wasn't hooked up to anything at all, of course. It was broken. But the lens pointed right at me. And it would have pointed right at Kiki, in that same spot there on the bed.

Sunlight streamed in through a slim crack in the curtains across my bedroom window.

It hit the power indicator LED just *so*, making it shine bright red.

SHIT.

seven

. . .

Kiki

THE BOTTLE of iced tea slipped through my fingers and exploded all over Mr. Skelly's newly mopped floor. "Shit," I muttered.

"Grab yourself another one, Kiki, and don't worry about it. Did you cut yourself?"

"No, Mr. Skelly." I brushed a few drips off The Track Suit That Time Forgot, a loaner from Mrs. Skelly while all my smoke-damaged clothes got cleaned. Grabbed another iced tea off the shelf, baby-penguin-stepped backward to avoid the broken glass and the huge mess I'd made, and made my way up front to pay. "I'm so sorry about that."

After everything Mr. and Mrs. Skelly had done to help me out, I repaid them with a teensy bit more property damage. Typical Kiki.

Another customer dinged their way into the store. I set my iced tea on the counter and hunted around in my purse for my wallet.

"Afternoon, Laura."

"How's it going, Jack?"

"That's quite the haul you got there."

"Gotta get these tomatoes in the ground early. It's the only way I can get 'em to take."

A pleasant-looking lady wearing five kinds of denim rested a flat of tomato plants down on the pickle barrel up front by the cash register.

"One moment, Kiki," Mr. Skelly rooted around on the shelf behind him. And he pulled out a security camera.

I stopped breathing.

He handed it over to the lady. It was identical to the one Brock had inflicted on me last week in his bedroom.

"Is Brock gonna hook this up for you again, or do you need me to come over there?"

"No, no. Just needed to grab this other one. Brock said he'll put it up tomorrow after work. Last year's camera went and killed itself dead about halfway through the season. Lord knows those squirrels probably sabotaged it."

Oh no. My heart thudded hard in my chest.

"Vicious creatures, squirrels," Mr. Skelly said,

and they both nodded in agreement about squirrels being the worst.

I got a pang in the pit of my stomach. Squirrels aren't the worst. *I'm* the worst. "Are you Aunt Laura?" My voice sounded so slow, so far away.

"Oh, see? My manners fly right on out that door when I'm in the presence of two ravishing beauties." Mr. Skelly grinned. "Laura, this here is Kiki."

"Well, hi there. I *am* Aunt Laura. So nice to meet you."

Brock's Aunt Laura. I wiped off a clammy hand and extended it to the woman whose pajamas I'd worn that night. And stormed off in the morning after. A week ago, now. To the day.

Has Brock told her and everybody else in this town how I went batshit crazy at his house? Doesn't seem like it.

Because he's a good guy.

How good? Let's review: he's raising his son alone after losing his wife, saving women from burning buildings and then giving them a place to stay, obliging said woman—orally, remember? *Yes,* actually, some parts on me in particular remembered it very, very much, every hour of every damn day this past week and then some—after she throws herself at him in his kitchen.

And then driving her home without so much as

a disparaging word when she flips the hell out right in the middle of sex. That *she* initiated.

Not just a good guy: *great*. Handsome. Responsible. Understanding. Good cook. Great cock. Saved my entire life.

And he's installing security cameras at his aunt's house so she can catch wild animals in the act of tomato theft.

No. That camera had been on. Hadn't it? Now I wasn't so sure.

"Nice to meet you too." My mouth was still talking but the rest of me had died inside. "I'll see you around."

I couldn't have overreacted any more to a broken camera on the shelf of the kind man who had rescued me from a fire, bandaged up my bloody cut leg, listened to whatever bullshit I spewed while I drank an entire box of wine, and then proceeded to eat me out the next day after I threw myself at him. And who, don't forget, would have provided breakfast and who knows what else, the devoted love of a lifetime, probably.

Had I not completely lost my shit.

I headed out of the store and back upstairs to flop down on my worn out old loaner sofa, totally defeated.

To torture me a little bit more, my mind

conjured up Brock's head between my thighs.

Then I relived the moment when I planted my whole foot on his massive shoulder and shoved him backwards. I experienced the surprise in his eyes all over again. My stomach ached.

I had to do something. So I pulled out my phone and texted.

> Got these pajamas for you.

But I didn't even have his number. I got up and grabbed my purse and keys, and before I knew it I'd hopped in the old clunker Mr. Skelly set me up with last week.

Maybe I could drive by the fire station to see if he was there? His house? That would be really something. The stalked-turned-stalker.

The engine groaned and wheezed but it didn't turn over. *I* groaned. I got out and slammed the door and balled up my fists tight, on the verge of a tantrum, like a real adult, and I blurted out, "Son of a—"

"Old Man Skelly set you up with a real lemon, huh?"

My eyes met Brock's. His steely gray waffle shirt stretched tight over his chest. My body remembered how good it was to be held against that chest. He was halfway out of Mr. Skelly's General Store, a flat of tomato plants in one hand and an iced tea in the other, holding the door open for his Aunt Laura.

"See you later, hon," she said to him. "Thanks for all your help." She flashed me a smile that wasn't overtly unkind.

But I detected a hint of *bless your heart* in her eyes.

Aunt Laura took one more look at the two of us and then hustled over to her car to beat it on out of there so she didn't get smothered by all the tension.

"Hey. I was going to text you when I realized I didn't have your number." All the anger and the fear drained out of me. I was so happy to see him, I felt warm all over despite the chill in the air. *I'm sorry*, I wanted to say. *I was such an idiot for a dozen different reasons.*

Instead I said, "I've got your aunt's pajamas."

So now I feel stupid for this thirteenth reason.

"You forgot your iced tea." He held it out to me. I closed in on him and took it. Our fingertips brushed. His eyes searched my face.

"Hey—" I started.

"Listen," he said, at the same time. "I need to apologize."

He needs to…*what*?

"I'm so sorry. I moved too fast that morning. Your apartment had just burned down, and then I took you to my place and got you drunk, and put the moves on you when you were in a really bad spot."

"Whoa, whoa, whoa. First of all, *I* got me drunk. You weren't the one hitting the nozzle on Aunt Laura's box of wine every half hour, on the half hour. Then I saw a camera on your shelf while we were…um, and I thought it was on. And I flipped out."

"Kiki, you didn't flip out. You followed your instincts. That was the right thing to do."

"Right thing to do? I almost broke your nose with my front kick." I was flattering my self defense skills. We both knew I'd barely moved him.

He smiled, so kind in his eyes. "A reaction is a reaction. You were only protecting yourself. Better safe than sorry. I shouldn't have forced that much intimacy on you right after we met."

"Forced yourself on me? *I* kissed *you*."

Not only that. I'd stuck my hands down his pants and grabbed his impressive cock, and swirled the pre-cum around its head with my thumb in an infinity-shaped swoop on the underside.

It hit me: that's how long I wanted to spend with him.

Forever.

His eyes brightened, fixed on me. He swallowed hard, bit his bottom lip, and then leaned in. "I know you did. I just wanted to hear you say it. Kiki, I...I like you."

I appreciated that he was careful with his words. But I could tell by the way he looked at me now, the way he had carried me out of the fire that first night, and held me close to his chest. The way he'd taken me home with him, and talked, and listened to me all night. The way he'd cooked way too much bacon for me the next morning. The way he'd buried his mouth deep inside me with wild abandon. And then the way he'd stopped when I demanded, and driven me home without protest.

I knew he loved me.

"I like you too, Brock. And I would do it again. I mean, I hope we...you'll—"

I couldn't find the words for everything I wanted to do with him. Because I loved him too.

"Really?" His eyes reflected all the love in my heart right back. "Do you promise?"

He set down the tomatoes in time for me to wrap my arms around his neck. His arms circled my waist and pulled me in tight.

"I promise," I said, and I pressed my lips against his.

eight

. . .

Brock

"HEY, HOW'S YOUR NEW GIRLFRIEND?" Cort's smirk loomed above my locker door. Kiki and I *had* been dating for three weeks now. But I didn't know if she wanted it blabbed to the whole town, so I kept my mouth shut.

"Take it easy, bro. Just because I rescued a woman from a burning building doesn't mean we're dating. I'm not *you*." I pulled on my shirt and checked my reflection in the locker mirror. I wanted to look good for her.

Plus, I couldn't ask her to be my girlfriend until Ben met her. Tonight was the night. T-minus two hours until I picked up Kiki and took her over to my folks' place for dinner.

Cort laughed and slammed his own locker shut, proud to be the subject of at least 90% of the town's gossip. People used to talk about him because he was the town junky. Until he achieved the biggest personal turnaround East Greenwich had ever seen. Got clean. Stayed clean. Started working out. Joined the fire department.

Now they talked about him because he saved lives.

And because he had dated nearly every single woman in town, and a few not-so-single ones besides. "Gemmie said if the guy across the street hadn't called it in when he did, she would've been one toasted marshmallow."

Across the street from Old Man Skelly's? Bella's old place. The only short-term rental in East Greenwich. "Who's over there these days?"

"I dunno, some out of towner from New York. Moved in a little bit after your girl got here, I heard."

"Oh yeah, who told you? Bella?"

"Not sure. I think Old Man Skelly mentioned it."

"And that's who called in the fire? The new guy across the street?"

"Yep. He's the one. Reported a bed on fire, Gemmie said."

What's some new guy from the city doing

sitting around staring into Kiki's bedroom window at night?

I left the fire station in a hurry and headed over to Skelly's store on my way home. Kiki was back to her original apartment already, all aired out and steam-cleaned and double-painted after the smoke damage. I'd see her in a couple of hours.

Maybe that wasn't soon enough.

Maybe she's living across the street from her stalker.

The hair on the back of my neck stood all the way up, and I had that feeling in my gut, like the one I got the night Hailey died.

The feeling that things were about to go all wrong.

I pulled into Skelly's. He'd raised the BACK SOON sign on the door. It was late enough in the day that I knew it was a lie. My heart beat harder. I called Bella.

"Why, hi Brock, so nice of you to give this old lady a call. I haven't seen you in an age. How are you? How's my darling Benjamin doing?"

"Hi there, Ms. Bella." Bella had been the recess assistant at Ben's school since I'd been a student there. "Say, quick question for you. What's the name of the fella who's renting your spot across from Skelly's?"

"Oh, have you met him yet? A little out of place around these parts. Drives that shiny car. Let me think. You know, at my age, it's not quite a steel trap up there. More like a big ol' strainer with them giant holes. Everything slips right through. Let me grab the check he gave me for the rental."

Papers crinkled on her end. "Must be under my duckie paperweight."

"How long's he renting it for?"

"Oh, 'round about two months. Said he wouldn't need it any longer than that."

My breath got more and more ragged in my constricting chest.

"When's the two months up, Bella?"

I already knew the answer. I could feel it in my whole body.

"I reckon it's nearly done now, Brock. Time flies when you're my age."

I had to get to Kiki, *now*. She was going to think I was a lunatic—*again*, showing up insanely early for our dinner date, flipping out over a feeling, a hunch.

But what if it's not just a feeling?

I shifted into reverse.

What if it's more than a hunch?

I peeled out as fast as my old pickup had in it to get going.

"Is this it? No, this is the check from my last tenant. I'm getting closer though, don't you fret. Say, why don't you bring little Ben around for some lemonade and cookies one of these days?"

"We'd love that." My voice choked with fear for Kiki. I clocked the vacant intersection ahead and blew through the red light.

"Here it is. Robert Walker. Like the actor. You wouldn't know anything about him, I suppose. That was before your time."

"Does it have his address?"

"Sure does. Says he lives on Park Avenue. Isn't that the fancy street with all the high-priced stores?"

"I'm not sure," I said. "I haven't spent much time in New York."

But I remembered every word Kiki said to me.

And I remembered that her stalker, Rob, the lunatic who rented her an apartment full of hidden cameras, besides buying a lot of properties with daddy's money, was also a douchebag hedge fund manager.

Who lived in a fancy place. On Park Avenue.

"Say, Bella, I need to go, but we'll be fixing to come see you. Real soon."

"I can't wait, Brock. Looking forward to seeing you boys." Bella let me off the phone without a hitch. Maybe she heard the sheer panic in my voice, or the roar of my truck's engine being pushed to the limit.

Sometimes this tiny little town felt like it was a hundred miles long. Finally, Skelly's other store. I pulled in and tore across the gravel lot, parked at the stairs to Kiki's apartment, and took the steps at a run.

Like the night we met.

Except now, the terror in me is unreal.

Now, I don't know if I've gotten here in time to save her.

I pushed that out of my mind and raised my fist to bang on the door, when I noticed the note stuck to it.

BRB
getting the good ice cream

The *good* ice cream?

It dawned on me. Where she'd gone.

My phone dinged.

The good ice cream. In Salem. The same convenience store where Hailey was killed.

I coded into my phone.

What flavor 🍦 would Ben want?

I dashed down the stairs and nearly collided at the bottom with Old Man Skelly, on the way out of his store.

"Skelly, who's living over there?" I tried to keep the rising panic out of my voice, but I couldn't. There's no shiny car over there, parked across the street. Bella's fancy renter, Rob from Park Avenue isn't home. And neither is Kiki. His lease was up. He'd been watching her. "Have you seen him today?"

"Well, now, what bee got into your bonnet, Brock?"

"Have you seen Kiki?" My legs froze to the spot where I stood. I couldn't get enough air into my lungs. Hadn't happened since Hailey.

I got paid to never panic.

"One question at a time. I'm not a young whipper snapper like you."

"I think Kiki's in trouble, Skelly." My voice went hoarse.

Skelly's expression grew thoughtful to match my fear. "The fella across the street? He did ask about Kiki, now that you mention it."

"Did you tell him anything about her?" I barely

restrained myself from grabbing him and shaking the words out of him faster.

"Hell no, Brock. What do I look like, Click-Clock? I'm not here to broadcast little info videos to every dang stranger who walks in this door. Miss Kiki and I did have a chat this afternoon. She said she was going to meet your folks and Ben tonight. Real excited about it. And she wanted to surprise him with that good ice cream she's heard so much about. So I told her the closest place to find it these days was the...store in Salem."

A shadow passed across Skelly's face after he said it, like it does on anybody's who knew Hailey. None of us go there. To Salem. To *that* store. Nothing wrong with it, nothing against the owners. What happened wasn't their fault.

You just don't want to set foot in the place where all the love and light in your world died.

I saw my Hailey's face on the pillow in the hospital—

Skelly said something else. But I didn't hear it.

"I gotta go," I blurted, and I hopped in my truck, gunned the engine, and took off towards Salem.

—the machines around her droned and beeped, everything soaked in that hospital smell, and little Ben: wailing, hysterical, searching for his mom's voice, her smile, each of us begging her, in our own way, to open her eyes—

God, Hailey, why didn't I come home earlier that night?

Only a few miles up the road was a tortured lifetime, and then there it was: that old clunker of Skelly's. Run off the road, windows up, windshield cracked, settled into the gully that runs off State Street. Next to it, a car way too clean and shiny to belong to anybody in this town.

And leaned down there on the passenger side stood the wealthy stalker scumbag from Manhattan who'd never been told no a day in his life.

Except by Kiki.

I pulled over and hopped out of my truck.

She was still in the car.

Her stalker turned to me.

"Hey there." He smiled, dead in the eyes like any psychopath. "Thanks for stopping, boss, but we're good."

I took a step towards him.

His smirk cracked, his eyes took on a twinge of fear. "I've got it under control. My girlfriend's having a little car trouble." He put his smug grin back on, pointed his thumb at Kiki and shrugged. "Women." He rolled his eyes. "Not the best drivers. What can you do? I've called the—"

Before he could think about pushing one more word of bullshit out of his filthy, lying mouth my fist was in it, on his teeth, his jaw, his cheeks, my knuckles split wide open against his shattered nose. He staggered back and I followed, my fists slick against his face and thrumming with their own distant sting upon impact.

I don't stop. All that matters is keeping Kiki safe.

————

Kiki.

She called my name from a far away place.

Kiki's stalker was a wet mass of bloody-faced mash on the ground. I'd really gone off. In my head, I could already hear Marmot's gravelly old voice telling me it was time to take a trip down to the station.

Then Kiki's hands were on my waist and shoulders and she dragged me away. I needed to see if she'd been hurt.

"What did he do to you?" I held her face in my hands and whispered so I wouldn't shout. My hands shook. I was still out of my mind with fear, even though she was right in front of me, alive.

"Nothing," she said, teary-eyed. She clutched

the edge of my shirt, hands balled into fists that shook uncontrollably when she released her grip. "You got here just in time." I put my hands around hers. Ice cold. The shock was getting to her.

I wiped my knuckles on my shirt so I could brush the tears off her cheeks without bleeding all over her face. She pressed herself in against my chest and I wrapped both my arms around her, as far as they would go. And I held on, tight. She looped her arms around me, her whole body shaking. So I held her tighter, until she stilled, and it eased the pain and fear in my mind, too. She was alive. I could breathe again.

"I thought I'd lost you," I said into her hair. I kissed the top of her head, reflexively, before I could stop myself. She craned her neck so that our lips met, and I kissed the tears from her face until our mouths found each other again. She slid her hands under my shirt and over my chest. It ignited my whole body, wanting her, and I hardened against my jeans.

Flashing blue-red lights illuminated her beautiful, tear-streaked face. I didn't look back. I knew who it was. Marmot hit the siren once, for good measure. We had a long history, he and I.

I snuck in one more kiss. For good luck. The patrol car's headlights illuminated a real mess on the ground. I'd gone too far. Remembering the night Hailey died, the fear of losing Kiki…it had driven me insane.

I'd have to plead insanity, if this human garbage didn't survive. If I'd murdered a man. Kiki'd told me she begged the cops to intervene when this filth had stalked her up and down Manhattan. And they'd done nothing.

Marmot's been my only experience of the law ever since he busted me for skipping class in sixth grade to go to the river on an awful hot day. He approached us, slow, boots clicking on the ground. Kiki wrapped her arm around mine, trembling again.

"Christ, Brock," Marmot said. "Didya kill 'em?"

"Sergeant." I nod. "Not sure."

"It was self defense, your honor," Kiki blurted out.

"I'm not the judge, ma'am." Marmot nudged Kiki's stalker's leg with the toe of his boot. The bloody pile groaned.

"Alright then." Marmot nodded. "No need to come down to the station after all."

He was the Sergeant who responded to the call about Hailey. Only that time, he'd arrived too late.

Kiki collapsed against me and heaved a sigh of relief. She burrowed her face into my chest and left it there. I wrapped my arms around her and stroked her hair.

"Skelly called me. Said I might find you between his shop and Salem." Marmot nodded towards Kiki. "Does she need an ambulance?"

"No," Kiki said into my shirt.

"Did your head hit the windshield?" I asked.

"No, only the, um, steering wheel. When he ran me off the road and into the ditch." Her breaths came in short gasps, and when she lifted her face, her eyes were glazed, shiny with residual shock and fear.

"You need anything more than that, Sergeant?" I rubbed her back and examined the reddening lump on her forehead.

It made me want to break her stalker in half, in many more pieces than that all over again, that he'd hurt her, that he'd traumatized her like this, and I turned back where he lay, immobile on the ground. But Marmot got himself in between me and him and waved me away.

"What about you? *You* need an ambulance? Any of that blood yours?"

"Not much of it, no."

He put a hand on my shoulder. "Brock, are you alright?" Marmot eyed me, sizing me up.

"I'll be okay." I was a wreck after Hailey died,

incoherent and broken. In the weeks that followed, I'd nearly needed to be hospitalized, too. My folks were so scared, they'd called Marmot to intervene. This wasn't *that*. But there were echoes of that old grief-turned-madness haunting my mind. I clenched and unclenched my hands, covered in blood. I hadn't known that about myself until now. "What about this mess?"

"Ambulance is on the way. We'll get him cleaned up and we'll get him the hell out of our town. I'll handle it. Nothing to worry about. Okay to run along then, you two. Take care of each other."

Kiki's eyes went wide. "We don't have to, um, come down to the station?"

"No ma'am." Marmot grabbed his canteen out of the patrol car.

He uncapped it and poured the water over my hands in a steady stream. I rubbed them together until all the blood had washed away and they were clean except for the raw split of my knuckles.

"Nobody in this town's going to jail for self-defense." He offered her the canteen, and she gulped down a swig of water.

You're safe now, I wanted to tell her. But I didn't know if she'd believe it from a guy who'd lost all control and nearly beat a man to death.

nine

. . .

Kiki

MY EYES DROWSED SHUT in the car. I struggled to keep them open, crashing after the adrenaline shot of being run off the road, recognizing him, the sick glee in Rob's face outside my car window—and then panicking so hard I forgot that cell phones existed, and that I had one with me in the car.

Brock had shown up right when I needed him. No call required.

"Are you okay?" He was still worried I had a concussion. But the crash hadn't been that bad. And I couldn't handle the hospital tonight...or, ever, really.

"I'm fine." I sat up with a start when I remembered. "What about Ben and your parents?"

"I texted them. Told them you weren't feeling well and we needed to postpone it to next week."

"They're going to think I don't want to meet them."

"Shhh." He took his hand off the gear shift to rest it on my thigh. "No way. They're not like that. I didn't want to worry them. I'll tell my parents the whole story in the morning."

"Your knuckles." The skin was swollen and rubbed raw in some spots and broken all the way open in others.

"I don't know what I would have done if you weren't okay, Kiki." He picked up my hand and kissed my palm, then the inside of my wrist, and set it down on his leg. At the stoplight, he turned to me and ran his fingers through my hair. His touch sparked an aching desire deep inside me.

But I wasn't sure he was seeing me, and not *her*.

I appreciated the gesture, and I wasn't going to shed any tears over Rob, but you didn't try and beat a man to death for a woman you'd met a month ago. There was more going on here than just us. I needed to know what.

My awful past was back there somewhere, either still laying in a ditch, breathing hard with his stupid face bashed in or being carted away in an ambulance.

But Brock's past was still in his head, and in his heart. Haunting him.

He pulled into the driveway and shut off the headlights. We didn't get out. We sat there and stared, silent. I knew he was in another place, another time. I had to ask him about her. I couldn't handle not knowing anymore.

"Will you tell me what happened, Brock?" To *her*, I didn't need to say.

His eyes, his whole face, shrouded itself in the worst kind of pain. He kissed the back of my hand again. "Let's go get some ice on your forehead." I wanted to object. I could tell he needed to talk about her.

And *I* sure as hell needed him to talk about her. But I let it drop and followed him inside.

He set me up in a comfortable spot on his couch, put my legs up, and settled my head down on a comfy pillow. "You don't have to do all this," I protested, but he shut me down with one incredulous look and threw a quilt over my legs.

"At least pour some peroxide on those knuckles before you do anything else," I said. "I don't want you to get infected from Rob's...botox."

"Was he *botoxing*?" Brock's mouth was a wide-open O of disgust and amusement.

"Yeah, all those Wall Street jerks do it."

"I thought something was up. His face didn't move right when I punched it."

I burst out laughing, and then Brock started laughing, and we both laughed until we cried, like we had that first night together.

"I can't believe I'm laughing an hour after getting attacked by my stalker."

"Stick with me, kid." Brock leaned over to kiss the top of my head. He wiggled the busted-open fingers on both his hands and winced from the pain. "I'm gonna peroxide these babies and then I'll bring your ice."

I *would* stick with him. Forever, if he wanted me to.

He noticed the blood spatter on his shirt and took it off, and I followed his bare chest and then his back with my eyes until he disappeared into his bedroom. He reappeared with that trusty first aid kit, like he did the night my place caught on fire, and sat down in the kitchen to rummage around.

"I was working late. Picking up an extra shift. Hailey was all alone here with Ben. He hadn't turned one yet. She needed more formula for him. And I'd completely forgotten to go to the store the day before. He was hungry. I wasn't around. So she went out, at night, all the way over to Salem to pick it up. She had Ben with her."

Everything in me wanted to go to Brock, to put my arms around him. But I was worried he couldn't talk and face me at the same time, so I stayed on the couch.

"It was the only violent crime this county had seen in decades. If only I'd been a better father, a better husband, she would still be—"

His voice broke, and I couldn't stay away any longer. I went to him in the kitchen where he sat and threw my arms around him from behind. His shoulders shook against me, but he didn't make a sound. Silent grief, the only kind of grief men were allowed.

I pressed my cheek to his hair and breathed slow and easy and held him. I didn't say anything. There was no reason to tell him it was okay. Because it wasn't. And it never would be.

We stayed like that a long time, until his breaths matched mine.

"Marmot—the Sergeant, the cop who came tonight, he got there not long after, but it was too late. She'd already been shot bad. She'd left—" His breath hitched, and he paused again. "She'd left Ben in the car. He was scared without his mom, crying hard when the police got to him. But not hurt. I rushed down to the hospital, and she—she was still alive. Barely. There was nothing they could do to save her. My life ended that night. I kept going for Ben, but every day since then I've thought about how the woman I loved died because of me."

"She didn't die because of you, Brock," I said, still holding him, pressed against his back where he sat. I let go, and I pulled up a chair to sit next to him.

"It was an accident. Her killer didn't even have a record. He was some messed up kid who had never committed a real crime. Panicked when she came in the door."

I eased the peroxide out of his hands, then shook it onto his knuckles. Watched the gore fizz up. He didn't register any physical pain, lost in the pain of his own past. "It's not like you were out at the bar." I blotted the blood off his knuckles, squeezed some triple antibiotic out of its tube, and daubed it on each split knuckle.

"But if I had been home that night, or if I'd done the damn thing the day before when she told me to, none of that would have happened."

I set down the gauze and gently tilted his chin towards me. His eyes couldn't meet mine. His face was full of anguish. And shame.

"You were at work, providing for your family," I said. But you can't argue away guilt. So I stopped talking and I kissed his tears away, one by one, like he'd done for me by the side of the road, until the crease in his brow relaxed.

Had anybody in this town taken the time to tell him it wasn't his fault that she'd died? It wasn't fair that the strongest people in this world were always left to struggle alone.

I stood up, and he flung his arms around my waist, buried his face into me. "I don't know what I would have done if I'd lost you too, Kiki." He exhaled a heavy sigh into me, his breath hot on my stomach through my t-shirt.

"I'm here." I ran my fingers through his hair. "You didn't lose me. You won't. Not now, not ever." The words were out of my mouth before I could censor them. I didn't want him to think I'd gone and picked out my wedding dress. But I couldn't hide what was in my heart. I kneaded the tightness where his neck met his shoulders on both sides until they eased.

He pulled away. "You're supposed to be laying down with a bag of ice on your forehead," he said. "And I'm going to make that happen."

He stood up and swept me off my feet in one motion.

I yelped. "What *else* are you going to make

happen?" I threw my arms around his neck. This was the distraction we both needed.

He carried me into his bedroom and lay me down on the bed. The look on his face told me *exactly* what he was going to make happen.

I was ready, wet, and all but begging.

He retreated into the kitchen and returned with an ice pack in a towel. I felt the growing lump on my forehead and winced.

"I hope you find head lumps attractive." I arched one eyebrow.

"I find exceptionally brave women very, very sexy."

He sat down beside me on the bed and lay the ice pack gently on my forehead. I sucked air through my teeth and exhaled through pursed lips.

"Sorry. Too cold? Maybe this will help." He leaned over and kissed his way along my eyebrow: slow, soft kisses that melted me from the inside out. "It's been a long evening, Kiki. You were run off the road by your stalker, and then…there was blood. And, your future boyfriend cried to you about his dead wife. Do you want to get some rest?" I appreciated the offer.

But his voice and his massive erection told me what he really wanted.

Time to show him what *I* really want.

"If you were my boyfriend, you wouldn't dare let me go to sleep without this," I rubbed the outline of his erection through his pants. "*You* lie down."

He grinned and complied. I threw off my bag of ice, suddenly totally healed. I unbuttoned his pants and struggled to get them down around his muscular ass and thighs.

Not to mention his stiff cock.

"Need any help with that?" He propped himself up on his elbows to admire my struggle.

"Wouldn't dream of it," I teased. He arched his hips and slid his pants and boxers down so I could tear them off and throw them on the floor.

"Wow." I took him in hand, knelt between his legs, and licked the roof of my mouth until it was juicy. Then I pulled my shirt up slow, to make him wait. He licked his lips.

I left my bra on so he'd have a minor obstacle ahead of him. I was nice, but I wasn't *that* nice. I wasn't small-town-*nice*.

I massaged the blood up his sculpted thighs and into his cock, moisture beading at its tip. I leaned over and took as much of it as I could into my mouth in one go, then sucked hard while I eased my way up, swirling my tongue around the tip.

Brock gasped, the veins on his neck visible all at once.

"Kiki, please—" He sat up and took my jaw in his hand, his eyes wild with desire.

"It's okay, babe. It's okay if you do." I wouldn't mind if he came right then, hard and fast in my throat. I knew he'd make it up to me with that mouth. I wondered who the last woman was in his bed.

In the future, I wanted it to be me.

"I want to be inside you. *Now*. If that's alright with you." He leaned over and pulled a condom out of the side drawer on his nightstand.

"It's all I want, Brock. All I want is you." I took the condom from him, tore it open, and eased it on him using my mouth, then rolled it the rest of the way down with one hand. I cupped his balls and leaned over to salivate on his tip, my eyes on his. I kissed my way up his abs and chest to lick and nip my way up the side of his clean-shaven face.

"Oh, Kiki." He pulled me down on top of him and I straddled his stomach.

Brock reached around and easily defeated my bra, unhooking it in one go and tossing it on the floor next to his pants.

Of course he did. My expert in everything.

I arched over him so he could suck on my

breast, tonguing my nipple until it stood on end. He turned to the other. I couldn't stop myself from rubbing against him.

"You drive me wild, Kiki," Brock's breath between my breasts drove *me* wild. "Ever since that first night. In that damn cat shirt."

I needed his cock inside me. I dropped onto the bed next to him and grabbed his shoulders to pull him on top. He kissed my lips apart, tongue on mine, parting my thighs with the palm of one hand. His thumb found and circled my clit. I moaned into his mouth. He increased the pressure until I cried out, gasping into his mouth on mine.

"I'm so wet for you, Brock." I slung one leg over his hips and guided him inside me. Didn't make it far. He was so thick I had to pause, panting.

"Are you okay?" He asked. "You're so tight, Kiki. Let's go slow." Eyes full of concern. "We have all night." He brushed my hair from my face and kissed my forehead, down my cheek, to my lips, biting at my neck. I lifted his mouth back to mine. I rocked my hips slow, back and forth, taking him a little deeper each time, my wetness slicking my thighs. I slid my tongue along his lips and I waited for him to exhale into me. Then I bucked hard and wrapped my legs around his waist.

Brock arched his neck and cried out.

"It feels so good inside you, Kiki. But I don't want to hurt you."

"You're not hurting me." I nibbled on his earlobe and sucked it into my mouth.

Brock pulled away. "Please don't let me do anything that hurts you." He took my face in both hands and looked deep into my eyes. "You have to promise me."

"I won't. I promise."

Brock inhaled sharp and pumped his hips against me. Then he lifted me up while still inside me and shoved a pillow underneath my ass, getting up on his knees and slinging my legs over his thighs. He slid into me again, opening me wide, and this time his thick cock hit my g-spot just *so*. He held my thigh against him with one hand, licked his thumb and set it up against my clit with the other, rolling into it with every stroke against my body.

The intense pleasure built inside me until there was nothing in my mind or my body except him and me and *this* and us. Brock increased his speed and pressure, pounding me at the perfect angle until I raked my nails down his chest and screamed out his name.

I panted my way into the afterglow, rolling my body against his and clutching at him with the dissipation of my orgasm, my whole body on fire. He ran his cheek along mine, sniffed my hair. He was still hard inside me.

"Come on me," I said.

"What?"

"Come on my chest."

Brock got a possessed look in his eye and then quickened his thrusts until he grunted and pulled out.

I missed his cock inside me immediately, but it was worth it to watch him ejaculate out of that thick, hard cock.

I pulled off the condom and propped myself up to suck his tip into my mouth the moment he came so I could taste his cum. Then I leaned back to watch him pump himself, covering my breasts with thick bands of his semen. I ran my thumb down my chest, painting myself in it, brought it to my mouth, and licked the cum off.

He knelt on the bed, panting, all muscle and sinew and sweat. "You're going to make me hard all over again, Kiki."

He lay down beside me and traced an infinity sign in his cum above my heart, then leaned over to kiss my mouth. I turned on my side and pulled his arm over me so he could be the big spoon.

As it turned out, I was, in fact, going to make

him hard all over again, according to his thickening cock against the small of my back. I gave him a devilish look over my shoulder.

He smiled and scooped up the ice pack off my pillow. "You melted it." He held it up, a bag full of water now. "You were too hot."

one year later

. . .

Brock

SHE PAUSED at the start of the aisle. My breath caught in my throat, and my heart thudded heavy in a way it never did when I was sizing up a burning building: wildly and completely out of control.

Her pause was too long. Was she having second thoughts? It had been an amazing year together, but she could have any man she wanted. She could move back to the city. Take up with some wealthy stock fund manager or whatever they're called.

Not some single dad firefighter in a podunk town. Like me.

I didn't think too hard about any of this when I got down on my knee six months ago. I only thought about spending forever with her.

She's so beautiful in that dress it physically *hurts*.

Did she regret saying yes? I'd wanted to wait a safe length of time to propose after her stalker showed up here in East Greenwich, after all the trauma she'd suffered—*we'd* suffered—from that night.

But I also didn't want to wait. At all. Because I knew then, like I knew the moment we met, I wanted to spend the rest of my life with Kiki.

She could be walking down this aisle in that cat shirt and she'd still be the only woman my eyes ever wanted to rest on.

Tears pricked at the back of my eyes. When Minnie started her piece on the organ, and Kiki took her first steps towards me, I couldn't contain the tears in my eyes any longer.

This year with Kiki had made my life *mine* again. After Hailey died, I put one foot in front of the other for Ben, but I didn't know how to live for me anymore. That first night at my place, when she laughed, and I laughed too, I recognized myself again for the very first time.

At the halfway point down the aisle, my mom walked Ben over to Kiki. My little man was the toast of the wedding, knocking it out of the park in a smaller version of my suit. He'd win a *who wore it better*, hands down.

"You look pretty." He said it so loud the whole church could hear. Never a shy kid.

"Well, thank you so much." Kiki curtsied to him. "You look very handsome yourself."

"I know." Ben grinned. The whole church broke into raucous laughter. We had some tough times after Hailey passed, but self-confidence was never Ben's problem.

He escorted Kiki the rest of the way, not a hint of nerves, only delight, scattering flower petals in front of her as she walked like we'd practiced.

"Am I doing good?" He asked her.

"Not just good," she said. "You're doing *great*."

"You're doing great too," Ben said, and he slipped his little hand into hers to walk her the rest of the way. "Here she is, dad," he called to me, beaming. "You can get married now."

I'm the luckiest man in the world.

bonus scene

. . .

Kiki

THE FIREFIGHTERS around his bed parted for me like they were the Red Sea and I was a bitchy, pregnant Moses.

"How *dare* you." I didn't care who heard me. The firefighters said abrupt goodbyes and scattered. "Yeah, I know," I shouted down the hallway after them. "You only run towards fires, not human emotions."

That turbo-slut Cort stopped on the way out and had the nerve to say, "He was so brave."

I put up my hand to stem his tide of bullshit. "Don't." I'd heard their macho lies uttered next to a half-dead man's bedside the year before, pretending the things they'd done were heroic instead of a stupid, hard-headed way to die. A stupid, hard-headed way to leave your very pregnant wife and young son behind—a child who had already lost his mother.

They had Brock hooked up to half a dozen machines that beeped and hummed and I couldn't help but compare it to when he'd had to visit his wife here. And she'd died.

Now *he* was here, and *I* was coming to see him. And—*and* I flattened my next hysterical thought before it drove me insane once again.

Like most of life's horrors, pure rage was the key to getting through this.

How *dare* he do this to me.

Leave me to work the night shift, leave me for two nights alone in my bed, in a small, vacant town that closes up shop by six every night, leave me and my hormones until I get a call in the middle of the night—

But he was awake. That fucking prick was wide awake. I pulled up short by his bedside. Not only was he awake, he was basically smirking at me, that son of a bitch.

I wasn't going to give this bastard the satisfaction of crying right now.

"How dare you try to leave this." I dragged the tears off my face with the backs of my hands. "How dare you try to leave me," I pointed to my swollen belly, my voice getting louder.

Brock had the audacity to glance at the doorway when a nurse poked her head in. Probably to see if she needed to call security. "Rhonda," Brock crooned, "Could you close that door for us? Thanks a million."

"You consummate bullshitter. Don't you dare take your eyes off me. How *dare* you try to leave *us*."

"Kiki—" I'd gotten too close to the bed. He grabbed me and pulled me up onto him, and for the first time I noticed the flimsy hospital blanket tented by his thick erection. "—now's not the time for an in-depth conversation about how I may or may not have died. You know I can't think straight when I haven't had you for two nights."

"What the *fuck*, Brock? Are you even hurt? Is this a prank?"

What was he doing hooked up to all these machines when he lifted me easily, like he'd just come from the gym and not had a burning building collapse on him?

"They're erring on the side of caution. I'm fine. Nothing a few painkillers and a shot of tequila can't fix. A little singed around the edges, that's all." He lifted an arm swaddled in bandages from wrist to shoulder. I straddled his legs, avoided his cock, and pulled the hospital gown up to see how far his burns stretched.

"'That's all'? What do you mean, that's all? Your whole fucking arm is burned, that's all? You almost died, that's all?" The bandages stopped short of his heart. I put my hand on it. "Is this not mine?"

"It's yours, Kiki. Never doubt it. I love you. With all of it, every moment of every day and night." He brushed my crazy thick hair out of my face. I thought it had been unruly before, but I didn't know wild hair until I got pregnant.

"So, then, okay. Great. You're not allowed to burn it in a fire. You can't fight fires anymore. I'm putting my foot down."

He didn't say anything, he only reached over and hit the button on his automated bed to raise the back of it up, his expression blank. Was he angry with me? It had never happened before. Then again, I'd never put my foot down before, about his job. About much of anything. I had no idea what he was going to say.

He didn't say anything. He yanked the hospital blanket out from under me and shoved it aside.

Then he unhooked his heart monitor.

And he lifted me up with both hands, pulled my underwear sideways, and shoved me down on his massive cock. A moan escaped me.

Fucking was going to ruin the silent treatment on my end, for sure. But I probably wanted it even more than he did, with all these pregnancy hormones running through me.

He pulled up my maternity dress over my head and threw it all the way across the room.

"Don't need that," he said. "You're so wet for me Kiki. I missed you. Two nights is too long." He rocked his hips into me, slow, holding me down with his hands on my thighs. I moaned harder. He stuck his thumb in my mouth while I bucked against him and made me suck it wet, then found the most sensitive point on my clit and edged back and forth against it. I gasped and clutched at him, gripped his hair in both hands. He took a nipple into his mouth, sucked on it, tongued it until I moaned again, louder.

I tilted my pelvis forward, bracing myself against his shoulders, and thrusted in time with him, his thick shaft hitting my g-spot. The pressure built inside me, waves of pleasure that overtook my whole body. I didn't know what toe-curling sex was before Brock. I squeezed my eyes all the way shut.

"Come for me, Kiki," he whispered into my ear, and drove his cock in hard, and it pushed me over the edge. I clenched around him, the orgasm tearing through me. I stifled myself by burying my face into the hollow of his neck and screaming through my gritted teeth up against his throat. He grabbed my ass with both hands and shoved into me—hard, quick thrusts. He growled low and muffled his mouth against my breast instead of calling out my name the way he would have if we were in our bed at home.

I panted on top of him, not in any hurry to kick him out, and let the sweat drip off my forehead for a good long while. I got cold and pulled the shitty hospital blanket around me.

He lifted me up off him and tucked me in next to him on his as-yet-unburned side. He kissed me all over my face, his usual post-sex ritual, and then licked the tip of my nose. Which was new.

"Yuck." I wiped it off with the back of my hand. Maybe the painkillers made him do it. Or the brush with death.

"Don't yuck my yum, woman." He slipped the oxygen back into his nose, put the heart monitor on his finger again, and replaced a few other tubes, cords, and wires we'd knocked off him. "I'll never quit being a firefighter." He kissed the top of my head, draped his burned up arm across my pregnant belly, and passed the fuck out.

And that's how I lost that argument.

also by maite maxwell

Need more fire in your life?

The East Greenwich Fire Co. Series

Barn on Fire - Everything I own is crammed into my Aunt Lucy's ancient barn. But I only care about one of those things.

Heart on Fire - I've had it with these know-it-all firefighters pushing me around. I've got a job to do, and no brushfire can stop me.

Pants on Fire - My livelihood is gone. I'm homeless. I have nobody to turn to. And I'm number one on the list of arson suspects.

Ship on Fire - This is my one chance to be free from my controlling mom and an Internet career she forced me into. But she won't let me go without a fight.

Tree on Fire - I'll do anything to save the Earth, one tree at a time. But he's the distraction I didn't know I'd fall for.

let's chat!

Ready for more?

Head to my website at maitewrites.com to subscribe to my newsletter for all the latest on your favorite firefighters and for a sneak peak into my next East Greenwich series.

And let's find each other on social media!

about the author

Maite Maxwell writes short, spicy, suspenseful romances featuring hardworking men and strong, passionate women who need a helping hand…and a little bit more.

On Fire: The East Greenwich Fire Co. is Maite's first series.

She's only had to call the fire department once in her life so far.

And they were very responsive.